Tortoise
Races Home

by Jill Atkins

Illustrated by Beccy Blake

Crabtree Publishing Company

www.crabtreebooks.com

Crabtree Publishing Company
www.crabtreebooks.com
1-800-387-7650

PMB 16A, 350 Fifth Ave.   616 Welland Ave.
Suite 3308,   St. Catharines, ON
New York, NY   L2M 5V6

Published by Crabtree Publishing in 2010

Series Editor: Jackie Hamley
Editors: Melanie Palmer, Reagan Miller
Series Advisor: Dr. Hilary Minns
Series Designer: Peter Scoulding
Editorial Director: Kathy Middleton

Text © Jill Atkins 2009
Illustration © Beccy Blake 2009

The rights of the author and the illustrator
of this Work have been asserted.

First published in 2009
by Franklin Watts
(A division of Hachette
Children's Books)

Library and Archives Canada
Cataloguing in Publication

Atkins, Jill
        Tortoise races home / Jill Atkins ; illustrat-
ed by Beccy Blake.

(Tadpoles)
ISBN 978-0-7787-3871-8 (bound).
ISBN 978-0-7787-3902-9 (pbk.)

        1. Readers (Primary). I. Blake, Beccy II.
Title. III. Series: Tadpoles
(St. Catharines, Ont.)

PE1117.T33 2009e   428.6
C2009-903989-3

Library of Congress
Cataloging-in-Publication Data

Atkins, Jill.
 Tortoise races home / by Jill Atkins ; illustrated
by Beccy Blake.
        p. cm. -- (Tadpoles)
 Summary: When it is time to go home after a day
of play, Tortoise challenges the other animals to a
race.
 ISBN 978-0-7787-3902-9 (pbk.) -- ISBN
978-0-7787-3871-8 (reinforced library binding)
[1. Racing--Fiction. 2. Turtles--Fiction. 3. Animals--
Fiction.] I. Blake, Beccy, ill. II. Title. III. Series.

PZ7.A86344Tor 2010
[E]--dc22
                                2009025299

Rabbit, Squirrel, Mouse, and Tortoise were playing in a field.

Soon, it was time to go home.

5

"I will race you all home," said Tortoise.

The other animals
laughed. "You are
too slow," they said.

9

"I will win," said Rabbit. "I can run fast."

"I will win," said Squirrel. "I can swing through the trees."

12

13

"I will win," said Mouse.
"I can roll down the hill."

14

Tortoise laughed.

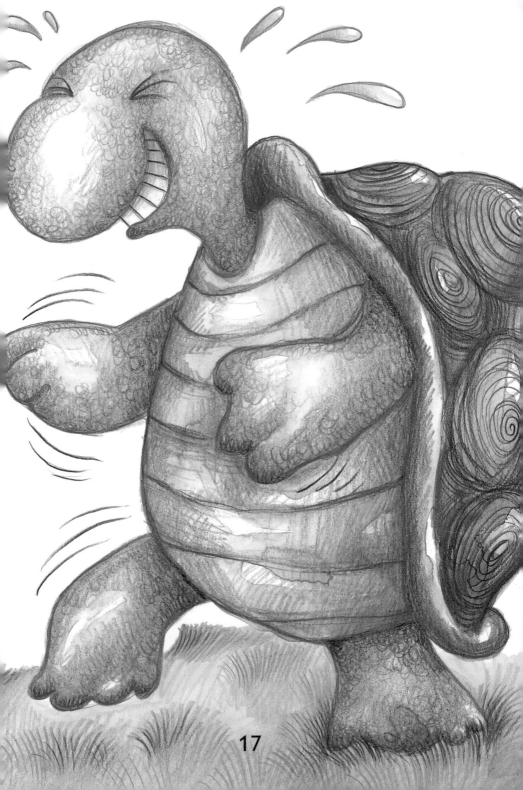

"No," he said.
"I will win ...

… because I am home already."

And he popped
into his shell!

Puzzle Time!

Put these pictures in the right order and retell the story!

clever

boastful

funny

surprised

Which words describe Tortoise and which describe the other animals?

Turn the page for the answers!

Notes for adults

TADPOLES are structured to provide support for early readers.
The stories may also be used by adults for sharing with young children.

Starting to read alone can be daunting. **TADPOLES** help by providing visual
support and repeating high frequency words and phrases. These books will
both develop confidence and encourage reading and rereading for pleasure.

If you are reading this book with a child, here are a few suggestions:

1. Make reading fun! Choose a time to read when you and the child are
   relaxed and have time to share the story.
2. Talk about the story before you start reading. Look at the cover and
   the blurb. What might the story be about? Why might the child like it?
3. Encourage the child to reread the story, and to retell the story in their
   own words, using the illustrations to remind them what has happened.
4. Discuss the story and see if the child can relate it to their own experiences,
   or perhaps compare it to another story they know.
5. Give praise! Children learn best in a positive environment.

Answers

Here is the correct order!
1.e 2.d 3.f 4.b 5.a 6.c

Words to describe Tortoise: clever, funny
Words to describe the other animals: boastful, surprised

If you enjoyed this book, why not try another TADPOLES story?

**At the End of
the Garden**
9780778738503 RLB
9780778738817 PB

Bad Luck, Lucy!
9780778738510 RLB
9780778738824 PB

**Ben and the
Big Balloon**
9780778738602 RLB
9780778738916 PB

Crabby Gabby
9780778738527 RLB
9780778738831 PB

Dad's Cake
9780778738657 RLB
9780778738961 PB

Dad's Van
9780778738664 RLB
9780778738978 PB

**The Dinosaur
Next Door**
9780778738732 RLB
9780778739043 PB

**Five Teddy
Bears**
9780778738534 RLB
9780778738848 PB

**I'm Taller Than
You!**
9780778738541 RLB
9780778738855 PB

Leo's New Pet
9780778738558 RLB
9780778738862 PB

Little Troll
9780778738565 RLB
9780778738879 PB

Mop Top
9780778738572 RLB
9780778738886 PB

My Auntie Susan
9780778738589 RLB
9780778738893 PB

My Big, New Bed
9780778738596 RLB
9780778738909 PB

Night, Night
9780778738671 RLB
9780778738985 PB

Over the Moon!
9780778738688 RLB
9780778738992 PB

Pirate Pete
9780778738619 RLB
9780778738923 PB

Rooster's Alarm
9780778738749 RLB
9780778739050 PB

Runny Honey
9780778738626 RLB
9780778738930 PB

The Sad Princess
9780778738725 RLB
9780778739036 PB

Sammy's Secret
9780778738633 RLB
9780778738947 PB

Sam's Sunflower
9780778738640 RLB
9780778738954 PB

Tag!
9780778738695 RLB
9780778739005 PB

Ted's Party Bus
9780778738701 RLB
9780778739012 PB

**Tortoise Races
Home**
9780778738718 RLB
9780778739029 PB

Printed in the USA---CG